Cake Test

To my aunt Maggie, with love

P.G.

For Weeda Wiseman x

J.M.

EGMONT
We bring stories to life

Book Band: Turquoise

First published in Great Britain 2007
by Egmont UK Ltd.
The Yellow Building, 1 Nicholas Road, London W11 4AN
Text copyright © Pippa Goodhart 2007
Illustrations copyright © Jan McCafferty 2007
The author and illustrator have asserted their moral rights.
ISBN 978 1 4052 2955 5
10 9 8 7 6 5 4 3 2 1
www.egmont.co.uk
A CIP catalogue record for this title is available from the British Library.
Printed in China.
44455/6

EGMONT LUCKY COIN

Our story began over a century ago, when seventeen-year-old
Egmont Harald Petersen found a coin in the street.

He was on his way to buy a flyswatter, a small hand-operated
printing machine that he then set up in his tiny apartment.

The coin brought him such good luck that today Egmont has
offices in over 30 countries around the world. And that lucky
coin is still kept at the company's head offices in Denmark.

Cake Test

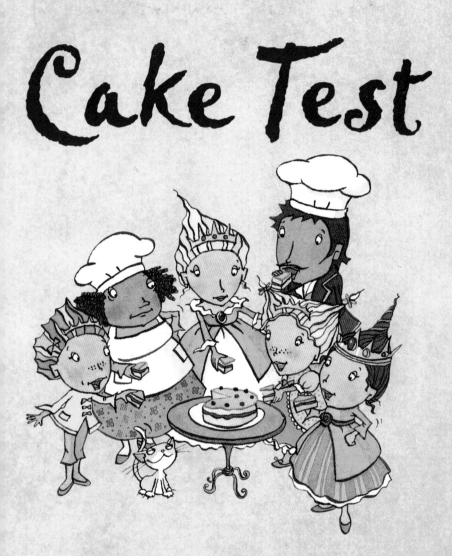

Written by
Pippa Goodhart

Illustrated by
Jan McCafferty

Blue Bananas

Baby Prince Frederick had a lazy

nanny who lost him.

Zzzz . . .

Baby Frederick crawled onto a road and nearly . . .

"Heck!" said Mrs Cook. "Whose baby are you?"

"Goo."

"Never mind," said Mrs Cook. "You come home with me."

Lazy Nanny told the king and queen lies.

He was stolen by the fairies!

So the poor king and queen never knew where their baby had gone.

In her little house, Mrs Cook
baked cakes and buns and pies to sell
in town.

As Fred grew, Mrs Cook taught him how to cook. She told him, "Follow what it tells you to do in the recipe and your pies will come out lovely."

Sometimes Fred got it wrong.

Mrs Cook told Fred, "Always add 'think' to any recipe." She was right. When Fred learnt to think as well as follow instructions, his cooking came out lovely.

Mrs Cook also taught Fred how to behave nicely.

"Bow down low if you meet grand ladies or gentlemen, Fred.

Always clear away your own plate and wash the dishes, Fred. That's my good boy."

Then, one day, Mrs Cook saw in the paper that the old king had died. She saw the picture of the old king and she looked at Fred. She saw what it said about the king's baby being lost.

Oo-er!

"Heck!" she said. "Fred, my boy, I think you must be a blooming prince!"

"Heck and a half!" said Fred.

So Mrs Cook took Fred to the palace and explained things to the queen.

"Frederick!"

said Queen Margery.

She hugged him and kissed him
and told him, "You will be the new
king!"

But Fred didn't know how to
behave like a king. He forgot he was
a grand gentleman now.

He was polite, but he forgot he was a
king.

Fred tried to be good.

But it was difficult to remember everything.

Don't do that, dear.

Queen Margery asked, "Whatever shall we do? He's hopeless!"

"He is *not* hopeless!" said Mrs Cook. "Fred learns everso fast, Your Majesty, if only you'd give him clear instructions."

Dear me!

So Queen Margery had a chat
with the Prime Minister and they
made a book of instructions for Fred.

"It's a kind of recipe for being a

king," Queen Margery told him.

How to Make a King

Take one boy or man of royal blood.

Wash to remove all dirt.

Wrap in fine clothes and sprinkle
with jewels to taste.

Place on a throne. Add one crown
to the head.

There were other instructions, but they didn't always work well. For example, "always eat with a knife and fork".

Heck!

Mrs Cook told Fred, "Remember, always add 'think' to the recipe!

Never say 'heck'. Say 'goodness gracious'."

Well I never!

As the months went by Fred got good at being a king.

"Time for Frederick to get married," said Queen Margery.

So Fred asked lovely Gwen to be
his wife and his queen. And one day
Gwen told Fred, "We're
going to have a baby!"

King Fred was delighted. Old
Queen Margery was delighted. Mrs
Cook was delighted too, but she had
some advice.

"Fred," she said. "Make sure
you get lots of nannies to keep your
baby safe."

"We will," said Fred.

It was lucky that they did because they were in for a surprise.

Waaa!

Nanny One came out of the bedroom and told King Fred, "You've got a lovely baby girl!"

"Oh, joy!" said Fred.

Out came Nanny Two. "You've got twins!"

"Goodness gracious!" said King Fred.

Waaa!

Then out came Nanny Three. "Another baby girl, Your Majesty. You've got triplets!"

"Heck and a half!" said King Fred, and he fainted, bump, onto the floor.

Nanny One put down Baby One and went to help the king. Nanny Two put down Baby Two and went to help Nanny One. Nanny Three put down Baby Three and went to pick up Baby One who was crying.

Baby Three began crying so

Nanny Two picked it up. King

Fred picked up

Baby Three.

Nanny One got some nappies.

I want
to see my
babies!

"Oh, they're all lovely!" said Queen Gwen. "But which one is the oldest?"

Ah!

"Er, we don't know," said Nanny One and Nanny Two and Nanny Three. "Sorry."

"Then which of them will become the next queen?"

Nobody knew.

The years went by and the

babies grew up.

Princess Cherry was sweet and

silly and lovely.

Heck!

Princess Hazel was sensible and
kind and reliable.

Whee!

Princess Apple
was clever and fun and
made people laugh.

King Fred was a good king. He used his book of instructions and tried to think as well. But Fred longed to do some more cooking. So he told the grown-up princesses, "I want one of you to be queen now, and let me retire."

But which one?

"I can do it," said Princess Hazel. "I've seen how you do the job."

"I'm wearing green which rhymes with queen, so it should be me!" said Princess Apple.

"Why not me?" said Princess Cherry. "I'd like to wear a bigger crown."

Me!

"Oh, dear," said Queen Gwen.

"We need to choose whichever of

you can follow instructions best,"

said King Fred. "Remember, the

new queen must be able to follow the

recipe for how to be a queen.

I'll give you a test.

Come on, girls, down to the kitchen."

"Right," said Mrs Cook. "Put on your aprons and follow the recipe and all your cakes will come out lovely. The best one will be used for the coronation party."

Not all the cakes did come out lovely. Princess Apple used the wrong kind of flour.

Princess Cherry used salt instead of sugar.

But one cake was really lovely.

Everybody liked Princess Hazel's cake because she'd made it with chocolate – yum!

Ooh!

Ooh!

"Hazel is the winner!" said King Frederick. "She's the one who remembered to add 'think' to her recipe. We will crown her Queen Hazel!"

Queen Hazel was a very good queen, and her sisters were happy too.

You're so clever, Apple!

But what about Fred?

Fred was happy baking cakes
and pies and buns. Queen Gwen was
happy helping him to eat them.
And together they wrote a new
recipe book.

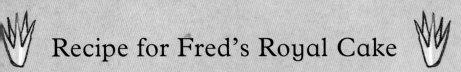

Recipe for Fred's Royal Cake

ASK A GROWN-UP LIKE MRS COOK
TO HELP YOU WITH THIS

What you will need

250g self-raising flour

1 teaspoon of baking powder

250g margarine

250g caster sugar

4 eggs, out of their shells and beaten

4 tablespoons of milk

jam or cream or whatever you fancy

for the decoration

You will also need a mixing bowl, a whisk,
a spoon, kitchen scales, one deep 18cm
sponge cake baking tin, and baking paper.

45

1)   Put on the oven to gas mark 3 or 325°F or 170°C.

2)   Grease and line the tin with baking paper.

3)   Sift the flour into the mixing bowl.

4)   Add the sugar, eggs, margarine and milk. Whisk them all together until smooth.

5)   Pour the mixture into the baking tin and spread it flat.

6)   Ask a grown-up to put it in the oven.

7) Bake it for about 30 to 40 minutes, then ask an adult to take it out to cool.

8) When the cake has cooled, take it out of the tin. Then ask an adult to cut your cake in half.

9) You can spread jam or cream or whatever you fancy on the bottom half before putting them back together.

10) Use your imagination to decorate it however you like. (You could even make fairy cakes!)

11) Share it with family or friends.
Yum!

PS If you want to make your cake like
Hazel's, then add a spoon full of sifted
cocoa powder to the flour.